Join the Cutiecorns
on every adventure!

Cutiecorns

Game Day

by Shannon Penney

SCHOLASTIC INC.

Puppypaw Island

FURMUSEMENT PARK

PLAYGROUND

BEACH

HANDYSNOUT'S HARDWARE

OUTDOOR THEATER

BARKING

FLASH'S HOUSE

FURBIDDEN FOREST

MISTYPAW MEADOW

GLITTER'S HOUSE

WOOFIN

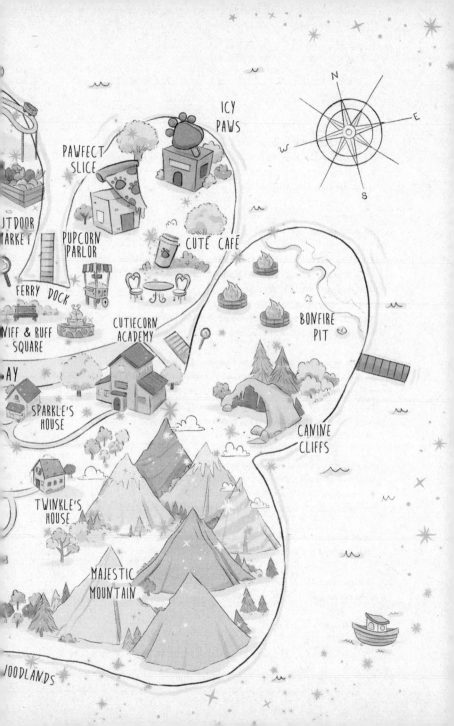

Text copyright © 2023 by Shannon Decker
Illustrations copyright © 2023 by Scholastic Inc.

ISBN 978-1-338-84710-9
10 9 8 7 6 5 4 3 2 1   23 24 25 26 27

Printed in the U.S.A. 40
First printing 2023

Book design by Omou Barry

Chapter 1

"Ohhh, it smells furbulous in here!" Flash cried. She pretended to melt into a puddle on the floor of the Pawfect Slice pizza parlor.

Her Beagle friend, Twinkle, rolled her eyes. "What a surprise, Flash is hungry," she joked.

Flash leaped to her paws and raced to the counter. Her tongue lolled out of her mouth as she peered at all the different pizza slices.

"What'll it be today, pups?" Bruno, the Bulldog owner of the Pawfect Slice, grinned at Flash and her friends. They visited regularly, and Bruno was always doggone happy to see them.

Flash scratched her head. "Can I have one of everything?"

Bruno chuckled. "You've always been a little pup with a huge appetite, but that might be too much even for you!"

Flash, Twinkle, Glitter, and Sparkle all ordered and paid for their slices—just one for each of them!—then plopped down in a nearby booth.

"Holy bones, I'm so excited for tomorrow!" Glitter, a white Maltese, said, waving a paw over her slice to cool it off.

"My big brother, Dash, says that Spirit

Week is one of the biggest weeks of the year at Cutiecorn Academy," Flash said around a mouthful of pizza. "It's going to be grrrreat!"

Flash and her friends were first-year students at Cutiecorn Academy. They weren't just regular pups—they were Cutiecorns! All the pups on Puppypaw Island had colorful horns between their ears that gave them special magical powers. The first-year pups were just learning to use their magic. Since they were new to Cutiecorn Academy, they were learning all the school's traditions for the first time, too!

Sparkle the Golden Retriever grinned, and her golden horn shimmered in the lights of the pizza parlor. "What do you think Spirit Week will be like?"

"I've heard there's a special theme for each day," Twinkle said. "I hope we don't have to dress up."

"Ooh, but dressing up would be puptastic!" Glitter said, clapping her paws.

Flash couldn't help bouncing in her seat. She felt tingly all over with excitement.

"I think there are different games and activities, too," Twinkle added. "They're designed to help us test our magic skills."

"Like Magic Tug-of-War?" Flash asked. They played that sometimes in class, and her strong shifting magic made her especially good at it!

"Sure," Sparkle said. "And probably some games we've never played before, too!"

Flash's mind was racing even faster than usual. She loved a good competition! Even though she was a first-year, she was confident in her magic and couldn't wait to put her skills to the test.

"How are we going to wait until tomor-rowwwww?" Flash groaned, fanning herself with her empty paper plate. "It's so far away!"

Glitter laughed and put a paw on Flash's shoulder. "I think you'll survive." She looked thoughtful for a minute. "I'm excited, too, but a little nervous. There are going to be a lot of surprises this week!"

Flash loved surprises, but she hadn't thought about how they might make some of her friends feel worried or uncertain. Glitter was always so good at helping her to see other points of view!

"Plus, we're the youngest pups at school," Twinkle added. "Everyone else has had a lot more time to practice using their magic."

Flash felt a bolt of uncertainty rush through her. Maybe her friends were right! Should she be feeling nervous about the coming week? She shook her snout to clear her head. No, she loved things like this! Surprises and pressure brought out the best in Flash. She understood why her friends might feel differently, but she still couldn't wait for every second of Spirit Week!

Flash leaped to her paws. "You three have some of the most furbulous magic of any pups I know!" She grinned at her friends. "No matter what, we're going to take this Spirit Week by storm . . . and have fun doing it!"

Sparkle stood up and saluted. "Aye-aye, Captain Flash!" she said with a wink. "Now, who wants to go play some beach volleyball to make the afternoon go by faster?"

Everyone headed for the door, but Flash stopped suddenly in her tracks.

"What's wrong?" Twinkle asked, turning to look back at her friend.

Flash grinned. "Oh, nothing. I think I just need another slice of pizza for the road!"

Chapter 2

Flash could barely hear herself think over all the barking and woofing that bounced around the halls of Cutiecorn Academy the next morning!

"Attention, students!" Mrs. Horne's friendly voice rang through the hallway speakers. She was the head of Cutiecorn Academy, and Flash and her friends had already learned so much from her. They were lucky to have such a pawsome teacher! "Welcome to Spirit Week! Please put your things away and join me and the rest of the teachers out on the front lawn."

Flash raced to her locker and tossed her backpack inside. As she slammed the door, Glitter jumped at the next locker over. "Flash! You scared me out of my fur! You were so fast that I didn't even see you."

Sparkle walked up, giggling. "If any of this week's competitions involve running, we're all in doggone trouble. Flash will have the whole school beat in no time!"

Flash grinned, bouncing on her paws. "Those older pups won't even see me coming," she said with a wink. She wanted to turn and dash off to the front lawn—she just couldn't wait to get there and get started!—but she took a deep breath and waited for her friends. If there was one thing she knew for sure, it was that friendship was more important than being first!

Together, Flash, Glitter, Sparkle, and Twinkle trotted down the hall and through the arched stone doorway. It was a pawfectly sunny day outside! Cutiecorn Academy sat up on a grassy hill overlooking Barking Bay, and the ocean breeze rustled the grass and nearby trees. Flash took a deep breath of the salty air. Her first-ever Spirit Week was about to begin!

Mrs. Horne and the rest of the teachers waved their paws in greeting from the other side of the lawn. They stood beneath an archway of colorful balloons, and streamers fluttered in the nearby tree branches. Flash and her friends joined the crowd of students and settled down, sitting on the warm grass with the rest of them.

Once everyone had arrived, Mrs. Horne clapped her paws for attention. "Welcome to Spirit Week!" A cheer rang through the air, and Flash resisted getting up to do a backflip . . . even though she really, really wanted to. "Every day this week will have a theme. Today's theme is Furbulous Fun Day! And we'll have plenty of fun today, I promise. But first, we have some other things to tell you about."

Mr. Magictail, a Chocolate Labrador teacher with a red horn, stepped forward. Flash grinned, thinking about how much fun she always had in his class. If he had something special to tell them, it was sure to be puptastic!

"This year, we're adding a new event to Spirit Week," Mr. Magictail announced, holding up a football in one paw. "At the end of the week, we'll have our first-ever Cutie Bowl! This will be a fun football game for any and all pups who would like to play. If you aren't interested, no worries—we need lots of enthusiastic spectators, too! Anyone who wants to participate can add their name to the list posted on the front door."

Flash couldn't stop her tail from wagging a mile a minute. "I'm totally signing up for that!" she whispered to Sparkle.

"I knew you would," Sparkle said with a

grin. "I'm going to sit this one out, but I'll make signs and decorations to cheer you on."

Glitter leaned over. "I want to be part of Flash's cheering section, too." Her eyes lit up. "Ooh, maybe we can make up some actual cheers!"

"Count me out," Twinkle said with a wink. "Cheers aren't really my thing."

"Oh, no?" Flash teased her friend. Twinkle was known for being a little gruff and grumpy, but she really had a kind heart and a great sense of humor.

Twinkle laughed. "Anyway, I think I'm going to sign up to play. I like football, and it will be cool to be part of the first-ever Cutie Bowl."

Flash couldn't help it. She threw her paws around her friend. "Oh, Twinkle, I'm so glad! I hope we're on the same team!"

"Me too," Twinkle said. "Otherwise, you're going to run circles around me on the field!"

Up front, Mr. Magictail tossed the football

to Mrs. Horne, who caught it easily in her paws. The pups clapped and whistled.

"Thank you, thank you," Mrs. Horne said with a smile. Her turquoise horn glimmered in the sunshine as she tucked the football under one arm. "I'm thrilled to hear so much excitement about Thursday's Cutie Bowl. There's a lot of furbulous fun to have between now and then, though, so let's get started!"

Flash could hardly sit still. This was it. Spirit Week was about to officially begin!

"To start the week off on the right paw, today will be devoted to a fan-favorite Spirit Week activity." Mrs. Horne looked over at Flash and her other first-year friends. "You first-year pups are in for a treat." She pointed at an older Dachshund student with a silver horn sitting near the front. "Duke, do you want to tell everyone what we'll be doing today?"

Duke jumped to his paws. "It's an obstacle course!"

course.

Chapter 3

This time, Flash really did leap up and do a backflip. An obstacle course! Bow wow, this was going to be fun!

"This isn't just any obstacle course," Mrs. Horne barked over the chatting pups. "This course will test your speed, agility, and magic!"

A teacher whom Flash didn't know—a Dalmatian with a dark green horn—whistled for attention. "We'll run the course in waves, from oldest to youngest. That way, the younger pups will have a chance to watch and see how this works."

"Well, that's a relief," Glitter said with a sigh, at the same time Flash cried, "Oh no! This means we have to wait so long for our turn!"

Twinkle and Sparkle burst out laughing.

Sparkle put a paw on Flash's shoulder. "Don't worry, I'm sure the day will go by in the twitch of a tail. There will be so much to see!"

Luckily, Sparkle was right. As the Dalmatian teacher led everyone around the side of the school building, the pups' eyes widened in wonder. A pawsome obstacle course stretched out across the grassy field. There were tunnels and walls and monkey bars and jumps. The course crossed over a babbling brook and even ran along the edge of the woods for a stretch. Paws down, this was the biggest, best obstacle course Flash had ever laid eyes on!

"Hot diggity dog, this looks amazing!"

Flash yipped, running circles around her friends.

Twinkle's mouth hung open. "Wow."

"Okay, now I'm excited to try this out," Glitter said, wagging her tail a mile a minute. "Look at all the different obstacles!"

The teachers led the crowd of pups to the start of the course and split them into groups based on their year. The first-years gathered on the sidelines with Mr. Magictail, barking up a storm. Music rang through the air as the older pups made their way to the starting line.

Before long, Mrs. Horne's voice echoed across the field. "It's time for the obstacle course to officially begin! First up: Dash. On your mark, get set, go!"

Flash jumped to her paws. She knew that

name—it was her big brother! "Go, Dash!" she woofed, watching as he raced across a narrow beam, used his magic to shift a ball from one bucket to another, and swung effortlessly across the monkey bars.

"Barking bulldogs, your brother is fast!" Sparkle cried, clapping her paws.

Flash grinned. It was true, Dash was fast—but Flash could still beat him in a race! He'd made her promise she wouldn't tell anyone, though, so her lips were sealed.

She whooped as Dash continued along the course, swinging on ropes that hung from the trees, finding a way across the stream, and moving through a shrub maze blindfolded. He finished furbulously fast! By the time he crossed the finish line, other pups his age had already started the course. Flash clapped her paws in appreciation—it was nonstop action!

As more and more pups worked their way through the obstacle course, Flash and her friends inched closer to the starting line. Glitter began chewing her pawnails nervously. Twinkle turned quiet and thoughtful. Sparkle studied the pups on the course. And Flash bounced around, unable to contain her excitement. It was almost her turn!

"Okay, first-years, you're up!" Mr. Magictail announced. "Dare I ask if you'd like to go first, Flash?"

Flash did a double backflip in response, and her classmates all laughed.

"I thought so!" Mr. Magictail said with a grin. "Step on up to the starting line. Mrs.

Horne will let you know when your time begins."

Flash put her front paws on the starting line, wiggling with anticipation. This was it! She was going to rock this course, she just knew it. And in front of the whole school, too!

"On your mark, get set, go!" Mrs. Horne barked.

Flash ran off as fast as her paws would take her. She crossed the narrow beam in no time, then used her strong shifting magic to move the ball from one bucket to the next, just like she'd watched her brother do. She zipped across the monkey bars, used her magic to open a freestanding door, scurried under a low net of ropes, and leaped across a series of tree stumps. When she came to a puzzle made up of twelve big, jumbled pieces, she used seeing magic to help her solve it in no time. Even though she was small, she had no problem swinging from rope to rope by the forest's edge or leaping up and over a low wall. She easily moved some log pieces into the stream using her shifting magic, then hopped across

with dry paws. Hot dog, she was moving so fast—and having so much fun!

Next up was the shrub maze. One of the teachers stood nearby and quickly tied a blindfold over Flash's eyes. She'd have to use feeling magic to move through the maze. No problem!

Flash stilled for a moment, feeling her purple horn glow. Following her magic, she turned right, left, left again. She was moving fast, eager to get to the finish line. She had to be close, right? The thought of it filled her with excitement, and she lost track of her magic for a moment. Suddenly, she turned—right into a shrub! Oops!

Flash spun on the spot, disoriented. Which

way had she been moving? Time was ticking, and she needed to get out of this maze!

She wanted to make up for the time she'd lost, but instead she paused and took a deep breath. As she did, she felt the magic flow through her—and suddenly she knew exactly which way to go. She ran as fast as her paws would take her, right out of the maze and across the finish line! Whew!

"You were totally pawsome, Flash!" Glitter cheered from the starting line, getting ready to run the course herself. Flash looked around to see Sparkle and Twinkle already out on different parts of the course. She didn't have much time to think about her own maze mix-up— she was too busy cheering on her friends!

It wasn't long before the very last pup crossed the finish line. Flash looked around at the exhausted, excited faces of all her friends and classmates as Mrs. Horne stepped forward.

"Congratulations, pups! I think this was our best obstacle course yet," she said. "You all performed brilliantly!"

All the pups clapped their paws.

"Now I'm very pleased to announce the winners of this year's Spirit Week obstacle course," Mrs. Horne went on. "In third place, we have Dash!"

Flying fur balls! Flash cheered so loudly for her big brother that she thought she might lose her bark. Dash took a big, silly bow and grinned from ear to ear.

"In second place," Mrs. Horne continued, "and keeping it in the family—Flash!"

Sparkle, Twinkle, and Glitter all squealed with joy, piling on top of Flash in a huge group hug. Flash could hardly believe her ears. She knew she'd been fast, but so many of these pups were so much older and bigger than her—plus, she'd gotten mixed up and lost some time. Holy bones, this was amazing!

"And in first place, congratulations to Roxy!" Mrs. Horne said, gesturing to a third-year Sheltie with brown-and-white fur and a bright pink horn.

All the pups stomped and clapped as Roxy smiled shyly.

Mrs. Horne raised a paw for attention.

"Now, even though it's Spirit Week, we do have some classes to get to. Enjoy the rest of your day, pups!"

As Flash and her friends followed the crowd back into the school building, Flash felt like she was floating. This week was off to a barking good start!

Chapter 4

"Glitter, I hardly recognized you!" Flash said with a laugh.

Glitter spun in a circle, showing off her new look. Her normally white fur was striped in all colors of the rainbow, from ears to tail! "Since it's Crazy Fur Day, I decided to put my favorite fur chalk to the test."

"I'd say it passed with flying colors," Sparkle said, winking.

Twinkle groaned and slapped a paw to her forehead.

The four friends trotted down the road to school together, just like every morning—but looking a little wackier this time! Flash's dad had helped her arrange her fur into pointy spikes. She felt like a giant hedgehog! Sparkle had the golden fur around her face all puffed out like a lion, and Twinkle had added some colorful glitter to her fur, so she shimmered in the morning sunlight. Flash couldn't help giggling every time she glanced over at her friends. They were quite a sight all together!

As they approached Cutiecorn Academy, the pups could see other students streaming

into the building. Everyone looked pawsome! Flash felt a warm glow run through her. She loved Spirit Week so much already, and it was only Tuesday!

After putting their backpacks in their lockers, Flash and her friends headed for the courtyard behind the school and found seats on the bleachers. Mrs. Horne stood on a little stage in front of them.

Flash burst out laughing. "Look at Mrs. Horne's fur!"

The head of Cutiecorn Academy had put big, blue polka dots all over her gray-and-white Husky fur. The dots matched her horn perfectly!

"Looks like Mrs. Horne has the same fur chalk as me," Glitter said, giggling.

"Good morning, students! Welcome to Day Two of Spirit Week." Mrs. Horne peered out at them. "Too bad none of you decided to do anything crazy with your fur today."

Everyone laughed. They all looked wacky, and they knew it!

"Now, I know you're eager to hear what

we'll be up to today," Mrs. Horne continued. "And you're in luck—it's time for a schoolwide scavenger hunt!"

The pups all burst out in excited barks. A scavenger hunt! Bow wow!

"You'll each receive a list of five items to track down, both inside and outside the school. Every list is different!" Mrs. Horne explained. "You'll need speed, smarts, and magic to locate your items. Once you find each one, touch it with your paw. Then use your magic to draw a check mark next to that item on your list."

Flash felt a sudden flutter of nerves zip through her. The first-year students were only just learning to use their magic to write on paper—and it was doggone hard!

Glitter put a paw on her shoulder. "Don't

worry, Flash. Your magic writing skills have gotten so good lately! All you need to do is focus."

Flash felt herself relax. Glitter had amazingly strong caring magic. She always knew just what to say to make her friends feel better!

The next few minutes were an exciting blur as teachers handed out lists to all the pups. Before Flash knew it, Mrs. Horne was blowing a whistle and they were all racing off in different directions. The hunt was on!

Flash glanced down at her list, trying to stay calm and collected. She needed to find a winter hat, a tall sunflower, a stone bigger than her paw, a measuring tape, and a container of apple cider. Easy-peasy!

She decided to tackle the outdoor items

first, so she raced to the school garden. Even from far away, she could see the bed of towering sunflowers swaying in the breeze . . . but she had to touch one before she could mark it off her list. She ran toward them as fast as her paws would take her! Flash tapped the stem of the tallest sunflower gently, then took a deep breath. Finding the flower was the easy part—now she had to mark it off her list!

She closed her eyes for a moment, listening to the far-off barks of the other pups. She could do this! Like Glitter said, all she had to do was focus.

Flash felt her purple horn begin to glow, and magic warmed her like a cup of warm tea. She stared at the list in her paw, concentrating hard. After a moment, a glittering purple

check mark appeared next to the words TALL
SUNFLOWER.

Flying fur balls, she had done it! Flash
leaped into the air and let out a cheerful yip.
Nothing could stop her now!

Feeling more confident than ever, Flash
darted off to find the rest of the items on her

list. All the stones that made up the school building were much bigger than her paw, so that was an easy one. She tracked down a container of apple cider in the cafeteria refrigerator and found a winter hat after digging through the Lost and Found box in the front office.

Each time, she made her body and mind very still and focused all her energy on drawing a magical check mark on her list. And each time, it worked!

Now Flash just had one item left to find: a measuring tape. She thought for a moment. They usually used rulers in math class. Where would she find a measuring tape? Suddenly, she knew: shop class! First-year students didn't take shop, but Flash had heard all about it from her big brother, Dash. Pups used all sorts of tools, along with their magic, to build incrediwoof things from scratch!

Flash ran through the hallways, barking and waving to friends she passed along the way. When she reached the shop class, she could hardly believe her eyes! The classroom was huge, with large tables in the center and shelves of large tools all around the edges. The wall next to the door was lined with a pile of wooden beams, which looked like they'd just recently arrived for a project.

"Holy bones," Flash breathed. "This place is amazing!" She began searching the room for a measuring tape, but she couldn't find anything that small among the different saws, sanders, paint cans, and mallets. There had to be a closet for smaller tools . . . but where?

Flash scanned the walls, looking for a closet door. She noticed the top of a door-frame behind the pile of wooden beams. The wood was blocking the closet—no wonder she hadn't been able to find it!

"Time for a little magic," Flash said with a grin, rubbing her paws together. She'd never shifted anything quite as big as this pile of wood before, but she knew she could do it!

Concentrating with all her might, she focused on her magic. She felt herself shaking with the effort, but slowly, slowly, the whole pile of wood lifted slightly into the air. Flash gritted her teeth as the wood inched to the right, until it was finally away from the closet door. Flash tried to lower it gently to the ground, but she was worn out. The wood fell into a pile with a loud clatter.

"Whoops!" Flash said with a nervous giggle. She'd come back to that in a minute. For now, she used a shaking paw to open the closet door. Sure enough, there were all sorts of smaller tools inside—hammers, wrenches, screwdrivers, pliers, and even measuring tapes! Puptastic!

Flash quickly tapped a measuring tape, used her magic to check it off, and breathed a big sigh of relief. She had done it! Now she just had to get back to the courtyard and turn in her finished list.

She closed the closet behind her. But as she

turned to face the classroom door, she felt a sinking feeling in her stomach. She had moved the wood pile right in front of the exit! Flash took another deep breath. She'd just have to move the pile back.

But after a minute, Flash knew she was in trouble. She couldn't get the beams to budge. She was doggone tired—and now she was trapped!

Chapter 5

"Think, Flash, think!" she muttered out loud to herself. There had to be a way out of this classroom. She couldn't move the big pile of wood all at once . . . but maybe she could move the beams one by one!

Concentrating hard, Flash used her magic to move one beam away from the door, then another, and another. Hot dog, this was hard work! Finally, there was just one beam left when the door handle rattled.

"Hey, it won't open! Hello?" a voice woofed from the other side of the door.

Barking bulldogs! Flash had to move that final beam, and fast, before anyone found out what had happened!

Shaking with effort, Flash tried to use her magic to slide the last beam over, but it wouldn't budge. Panicked, she raced over to the beam, put her paws on it, and pushed with all her might until it moved clear of the doorway. The door burst open and a Chihuahua with a purple horn came into the room.

"Oh, hi!" she said, surprised. "I didn't know there was anyone in here. I was having trouble with the door!"

Flash tried to look confused. "That's so weird! I wonder if the handle was stuck." She shrugged and gave the pup a friendly wave. "Anyway, gotta go—good luck with your scavenger hunt!" Without another word, she bolted out the door and down the hall.

When she finally stopped to catch her breath, Flash felt terrible. She had lied to that other pup! She just couldn't bear the thought of anyone finding out that she'd gotten herself trapped in the wood shop. It was so embarrassing! That was the first time that her shifting magic hadn't worked quite right. Was her magic really as strong as she'd thought?

The rest of the day passed in a blur of crazy fur, classes, and Spirit Week fun. Teams were assigned for Thursday's Cutie Bowl, and Flash was puptastically excited to be on the same team as Twinkle. But in the back of her mind, she couldn't stop thinking about her magic mistake that morning. She felt rattled . . . fur real!

That night, Flash cuddled up under her covers with a book—one of her favorites, about puppy pirates!—and waited for her parents to come in and say good night.

Sure enough, her dad's snout peeked around her door a few minutes later. "Knock, knock!" he called. "Any sleepy pups in here?"

"Nope, sorry!" Flash said with a giggle. "I have all the energy in the—" But before she could finish her sentence, she let out a big yawn.

"Even our Flash gets tired sometimes," her mom said, walking in behind her dad and giving Flash's paw a squeeze.

"How was Crazy Fur Day?" Flash's dad asked. "I hope you didn't impale anyone with your fierce spikes." He winked. He had helped Flash gel her fur into pointy spikes that morning, and he loved to joke about what a dangerous look it was.

"Oh, it was good," Flash said. "We had a scavenger hunt, and we had to use our magic to help us find different things on our lists."

Her mom grinned. "That sounds like fun! I'll bet you were great at that."

Flash gave a small smile. "It was ter-ruff-ic, but it really put my magic to the test."

She saw her parents exchange a glance. Her dad sat down on the edge of her bed. "Here's a quick bedtime story. Have I ever told you about the time I was out at sea, sailing to Reindeer Reef?"

Flash shook her head. Her dad was an explorer, so he was full of exciting tales, but she didn't think she'd heard this one before! She sat up in bed—she was all ears!

"Reindeer like cold weather, so it was a long, chilly trip," Flash's dad explained. "I was doggone tired, and my magic wasn't working the way it should. At one point, I was down on the deck, adjusting one of the sails, when I spotted a big chunk of ice straight ahead of my boat! I wasn't sure I had time to get to the helm to grab the wheel, so I decided to use my shifting magic to turn the wheel. But I was so tired that it wasn't working!"

Flash grabbed her dad's paw. "Holy bones, Dad! What did you do?" She was glad her dad was here now, because that meant his story turned out all right.

"I raced to the helm as fast as my paws

would take me and grabbed the wheel!" he explained. "My magic was strong, but I just didn't have it in me that day. Luckily, I thought fast and was quick on my paws."

Flash's mom smiled. "I know someone else who thinks fast and is quick on her paws," she said, giving Flash a big hug. "Now it's time for you to rest up. Tomorrow is a new day!"

Flash squeezed both of her parents tight, flipped off her light, and snuggled down under her blankets again. This time, she felt warm, cozy, and comforted. Even her dad made mistakes with his magic sometimes, and he was the boldest, bravest pup she knew!

Her mom was right—tomorrow was a new day, and Flash was going to be ready for it!

Chapter 6

"It's Day Three of Spirit Week," Mrs. Horne announced in the school auditorium the next morning. "Today is Maximize Your Magic Day!"

Flash wiggled in her seat. They'd practiced making their magic big in class before, and it was always a puptastic time!

"We have a variety of games and activities

set up outside. You get to choose what you'd like to try!" A cheer went up from the crowd, and Mrs. Horne smiled. "You can do one game or all of them, but the main goal of each is to make your magic as big as possible."

Mr. Bowser, the Greyhound PE teacher, stepped forward. "Outside, you'll find stations for karaoke, dodgeball, a dance-off, Frisbee, and trivia." He blew his coaching whistle and the pups all jumped in surprise. "Time to go maximize your magic!"

Flash leaped to her paws. "What are you going to do first?" she asked her friends eagerly.

"Dodgeball!" Twinkle said without hesitating.

"Frisbee!" Sparkle woofed. Flash knew that

she could jump really high and make some amazing catches!

Glitter smiled shyly. "I think I'd like to check out the trivia."

Flash thought for a moment. "I'm going to try the dance-off," she said. "I have some big ideas for how to use my magic there!"

"What a surprise!" Twinkle joked, nudging Flash's shoulder.

All four pups headed outside to the field. It looked even more fun and festive than it had earlier in the week! With so many different activities happening, the energy was high.

Flash could hear upbeat music around the corner. "Bow wow, that's my favorite song!" she cried. "I'm going to go check it out."

Waving goodbye to her friends, Flash took off running. As she skidded around the corner, she saw an older pup dancing on a big platform. She'd found the dance-off!

Flash couldn't help herself—she did an excited backflip in the air. She had done more backflips this week than in the whole rest of the school year put together! She raced to the side of the platform, where a small group of pups was waiting for their turn to dance. She watched eagerly as they took the stage one by one to show off their best moves.

Here, too, the pups used their magic in special ways. One break-dancing Bulldog spun on his back so fast that she was just a blur. A Terrier leaped higher than any ballerina Flash had ever seen. A tap-dancing Poodle used his

magic to amplify the sound of his tapping—it was even louder than the music!

As Flash waited her turn, she thought about how to use her magic alongside her dance moves. She knew her shifting magic was strongest, but what could she shift while she was dancing?

Then it hit her like a box of bones—props! Flash had seen some old musicals during movie nights on the beach. Those were always filled with singing and dancing that used fun props: umbrellas, canes, top hats, and more. Flash scanned the area for something she could use, and the answer waved at her from the nearby garden. A sunflower! Hot dog, this was going to be fun!

Finally, it was Flash's turn to take the stage! A song by her favorite band, the Magic Mutts, blared over the speakers. As she showed off her best dance moves, she could hear the crowd barking up a storm!

Flash moved faster and faster around the stage. She was really on a roll now! It was time to try out her magic, but she couldn't stay still—she had to keep dancing. Flying fur balls, she'd really have to concentrate! Flash glanced over at the garden and chose one specific sunflower, still dancing all the while. She felt her magic course through her, and her purple horn began to glow. It was working!

Or was it?

The sunflower was wiggling in place, but Flash couldn't get it to budge from the ground. She heard the pups in the crowd cheering her on. She had to make this work!

Flash focused on her shifting magic with all her might, and suddenly, the sunflower popped into the air and zoomed toward her. Bow wow, she'd done it! Flash flipped on the spot, spinning and dancing in celebration—until the

sunflower arrived faster than she had expected and hit her right in the snout. Ow!

The flower flopped down on the stage, dropping some of its petals, and Flash froze in place. She hadn't stayed focused on her magic, and she'd made a silly mistake in front of everyone! What ruff luck!

At that moment, the song ended and Flash left the stage to loud, cheerful woofs. But inside, she felt terrible. Was she going to be the laughingstock of Cutiecorn Academy?

Chapter 7

"Holy bones, that was the most epic dodgeball game I've ever been a part of!" Twinkle gushed as she, Flash, Glitter, and Sparkle trotted across the sandy beach after school. "You should have seen the magic some pups were trying out! Our team lost, but it was still a ter-ruff-ic time."

"You know who really had an amazing

showing today?" Sparkle said, nudging Glitter. "Glitter! She came in third in the trivia game—against a ton of older pups!"

Glitter gave a sweet smile. "I really like trivia. My mom asks me questions at dinner sometimes!"

Flash half listened as her friends all recapped the day's Spirit Week activities. She was happy for her puppy pals, but couldn't stop thinking about her dance-off blunder! No one had said anything when she left the stage, but she still felt awful. How embarrassing!

The four friends took off their backpacks and sat down near the water's edge. Flash felt the sun on her fur. She took a deep breath of the salty air.

"Is everything okay?" Glitter asked Flash.

Her pink horn shimmered in the sunlight. "You've been awfully quiet. That's not like you!"

"Oh, I'm pawsome!" Flash said a little too fast.

Glitter gave her paw a squeeze. "Okay. But it's also okay if you're not, you know."

Flash hung her snout. Glitter was right! She didn't need to hide how she was feeling from her friends.

"Well," she began slowly, "my shifting magic didn't work the way I wanted it to during the dance-off today. And no one knows this, but it also backfired during the scavenger hunt yesterday. I'm worried that something's wrong with my magic!" She buried her face in her paws.

Sparkle patted her on the back. "I saw what happened today, when you used your magic to get a sunflower all the way from the garden." The Frisbee field had been right near the dance-off, and Flash knew that Sparkle had come to watch when her game was done. "That was doggone hard, Flash!"

Glitter and Twinkle both nodded firmly.

"And you totally did it," Sparkle went on. "You just got excited and lost your concentration before you caught it, that's all. That could have happened to anyone—but most pups couldn't have shifted that sunflower in the first place!"

Flash felt a small smile stretch across her snout. Then her shoulders fell.

"But yesterday, I was trying to shift a pile of wood in the shop class, and I got so tired," she said gloomily. "I almost got stuck in the classroom because I was having trouble moving the last piece with my magic!"

Twinkle got to her paws. "Flash, are you telling me that you moved a huge pile of wood with your magic? And you're upset because it made you tired and you couldn't move one last piece?"

Flash nodded. "When you put it that way, I guess it doesn't sound so bad."

Twinkle laughed. "Not bad? Your shifting powers are incredible, Flash! Everyone gets tired or overly excited sometimes. That doesn't mean that anything is wrong with your magic!"

"Twinkle's right," Glitter said. "You just need to believe in yourself. Plus, we're all still learning. It's okay to make mistakes."

Flash felt all warm inside. Her friends knew exactly how to make her feel better! She was the luckiest pup in the world to have Sparkle, Glitter, and Twinkle as best buddies.

"Now, I want to hear more about this

dance-off," Twinkle said. "What kind of dancing did—whoa!"

At that moment, a big wave crested in front of them. When it splashed down, they were going to get soaked—and there wasn't time for them to scramble to their paws and jump out of the way!

Without thinking, Flash felt magic course through her. The purple glow from her horn glimmered in the afternoon sunlight. Before she even knew what she was doing, Flash used her shifting magic to part the water in front of them. It splashed on either side of the four friends, but they stayed completely dry.

As the water receded, Glitter, Sparkle, and Twinkle turned to look at Flash with wide eyes. All four pups were silent.

Suddenly, Flash's friends howled with excitement.

"How did you do that?"

"Flash, that was puptastic!"

"See? Your shifting magic is stronger than ever!"

Flash laughed. Her friends' enthusiasm was contagious!

"I guess you guys were right," she said, a smile stretching across her snout. "My shifting magic seems to be okay!"

Twinkle rolled her eyes dramatically. "That's the biggest understatement I've ever heard!" She got to her paws and looked at Flash. "So now that we know your magic is okay, let's make sure you haven't lost your speed. Race you to the dock and back!" Without waiting, Twinkle took off down the beach, her paws pounding on the sand.

Flash leaped up and raced after her friend. "Lose my speed?" she barked with a laugh. "Never!"

Chapter 8

"Welcome, one and all, to the first annual Cutie Bowl!"

Mrs. Horne's bark echoed over the loudspeaker, and a roar of cheers went up around Cutiecorn Academy's football field. The marching band played an upbeat tune. Flags and banners and balloons waved and bobbed around the field, like an explosion of color.

Standing on the sidelines with her team, Flash could hardly take it all in. The Cutie Bowl was finally here!

Flash could feel some game-day jitters swirling around inside her, but there was too much happening to focus on her nerves! She smoothed out the front of her crisp maroon uniform. It had a number 8 on the back, which had always been her lucky number. Flash was pretty sure that had to be a sign—she was going to have a pawsome game!

As the music died down, Mrs. Horne continued. "I'm thrilled to have you all here today. And now, without further ado, let me introduce our teams!"

Twinkle nudged Flash's shoulder. "Here we go! Ready to rock?"

Flash grinned. "You bet your bark I am!"

The Maroon and Gold Teams both ran out onto the field, waving their paws to friends in the crowd. Flash could see Glitter and Sparkle in the front row of the bleachers, barking their snouts off. Glitter held a shimmering sign that read PAWS OFF! THAT BALL BELONGS TO THE MAROON TEAM! in bubble letters. Sparkle waved a paw-made flag with Flash's and Twinkle's names on it, surrounded by hearts, stars, and big "#1"s. Flash did a silly dance move and waved to them. She was lucky to have the best friends a pup could ask for, and she knew it!

"Watch out for my little sister over there," Flash could hear Dash telling his Gold teammates nearby. "She's fast!" He winked at her

and gave her an encouraging smile. Even though they were on opposite teams, Flash knew her brother was rooting for her!

"Get in position, pups!" Mr. Magictail had taken over the microphone now that the game was about to begin. Flash, Twinkle, and the rest of their teammates rushed to their assigned spots on the field. Flash's tail wagged in excitement as the whistle blew. It was game time!

Flash tried to block out all the sights and sounds around her, and focus on what was happening on the field. Barking Bulldogs, that was easier said than done! There were so many distractions. But after a few minutes, Flash found her stride. She watched as the older pups on the Gold Team took control of the ball, and cheered wildly as Twinkle intercepted it during a pass. Twinkle's seeing magic really came in handy during games like this, Flash knew. She could use it to understand others better and anticipate what kinds of things they might do!

For Flash's part, she moved around the field

as fast as lightning. She chased down receivers so they got distracted and missed their catches. If there was one thing Flash knew she could always rely on, it was her speed!

For a while, the game stayed scoreless. But then Flash saw her big brother racing toward the end zone, and she knew she had to stay right on his tail. She ran as fast as her paws would take her, and had almost caught up to him when he leaped into the air, snagged the football, and scored.

"And Dash scores for the Gold Team!" Mr. Magictail announced cheerfully, as the crowd erupted in both cheers and boos.

Flash kicked the ground in frustration. She'd been so close!

Dash gave her a high paw on his way past.
"Keep it up, little sis—you almost had me!"

"You know you won't get away with that
next time!" Flash called after him with a grin.
Her brother was right. She had to keep trying!

The game went on, packed with nonstop

action—and some surprises, too! Magic was allowed on the field, so pups tried out their fanciest tricks. One of the pups on the Maroon Team made the ball super-tiny while it was in midair, so the Gold receiver couldn't see it to make the catch. Another pup used magic to jump extra high and hover in the air so she could snag the ball from way above the field. The crowd woofed and cheered wildly with every play!

Even though the teams pulled out all the stops, Dash was the only pup to score a touchdown in the whole first half of the game. The defense on both teams was too ter-ruff-ically good! When Mr. Magictail blew the whistle for halftime, the Gold Team was ahead 7–0.

The pups trotted off the field for a break, and Flash flopped down dramatically on the sidelines. "I'm doggone tired!" she panted.

Twinkle sat next down heavily next to her. "Tell me about it! We've had such ruff luck out there. With all those magical moves, we should totally be winning!"

Flash nodded, but something Twinkle had said gave her a funny feeling in her stomach. Flash hadn't used any magical moves in the whole first half of the game! She'd been too busy zipping around the field. If she had used her magic, would her team be doing better by now? But what if she tried to use her magic and failed? Her magic was strong, but it was hard to use when she was distracted or tired. Now she was both!

Flash sat up and shook her snout. She needed to do something in the second half to help her team. But what?

Chapter 9

Flash couldn't think too much about the second half of the game, because the band began to play an upbeat song as they marched out onto the field. They did silly dance moves and even made themselves into formations to spell out words and phrases like GO GOLD! and MAROON IS PAWSOME! all while playing their instruments! Flash was enthralled. But that was just the beginning . . .

As the marching band continued playing, the Cutiecorn Academy Dance Team took the field with them. Holy bones, those pups had some puptastic moves! Not only could they dance, but they could do flips, acrobatics, lifts, and tosses, too. Flash couldn't stop her paws from tapping on the ground! Maybe she'd try out for the dance team one day.

At the end of the show, the dance team pups did a spectacular pyramid and barked, "Both teams are grrrrrrreat!" as the marching band finished with a flourish. A roar went up from the crowd. Flash clapped her paws as hard as she could! She suddenly felt refreshed and energized.

Smiling, she turned to Twinkle. "I'm ready for the second half—let's get back out there!"

Twinkle gave her a high paw, and they bolted out onto the field alongside the rest of the Maroon Team. The pups took their positions, and the whistle sounded. Game time!

For the first few minutes, the ball didn't

move very far down the field. Both teams tried their hardest, but it was a pawfect matchup! After a lot of back and forth, the Maroon Team finally scored three points with a field goal kick. (Their kicker, a Rottweiler named Boots, was super-strong!) The score was 3–7, but the Gold Team was still ahead.

As the clock kept ticking, Spark, the captain of the Maroon Team, had the chance to pass the ball down the field. Only one pup was open—Twinkle! Flash watched as she leaped, grabbed the ball—and it slipped through her paws! Oh no!

Spark ran over to Twinkle and patted her on the shoulder, with Flash close behind. "Nice try," Spark said with a grin. "We'll get it next time!"

Twinkle smiled back. She didn't look upset at all!

"I'm sorry, Twinkle," Flash said softly. "That was ruff. You were so close!"

Twinkle shrugged. "It's okay! I did my best. We'll have more chances to score."

Flash felt a rush of pride for her friend. What a puptastic sport!

As she took her position on the field again, Flash started to feel braver and bolder. Twinkle was right! All they could do was try their best. So what if they messed up? No one in the stands was making fun of Twinkle. Instead, they were cheering louder than ever! Maybe something would work or maybe it wouldn't, but Flash would never know if she didn't try.

On the next play, Flash darted as fast as

her paws would take her down the field. This time, Spark threw the ball—and it was coming toward her! Flash would have to move fast to get to the right spot to catch it. Her paws pounded on the grass, but she couldn't seem to keep up. The ball was going to sail right over her snout!

Or was it?

Flying fur balls, Flash could do something about this. She was a Cutiecorn, after all—she could use her magic! But she'd have to act fast.

Concentrating hard and still running at full speed, Flash looked over her shoulder at the football. If she could just shift it downward, she could reach it with her paws. "Focus, Flash, focus!" she muttered to herself.

Suddenly, she felt a rush of magic course

through her. Her horn glowed a brilliant purple. As if in slow motion, she saw the ball drop
through the air. It was within reach!

Flash sprang off her back legs and leaped
high. The ball kept dropping, dropping . . .
right into her outstretched paws! She'd done it!

As she landed, she realized that her paws

were in the end zone. She had run so far and so fast that she'd reached the end of the field. Not only had she caught the ball, she had scored a touchdown!

The crowd howled with excitement. The marching band played a fanfare, and Flash looked up to see her whole team racing toward her. They hoisted her onto their shoulders and tossed her gently into the air in celebration. (She was starting to feel like one of those dance team pups after all!)

When Flash finally had all four paws on the ground again, Twinkle gave her a big hug. "No one but you could have made that play, Flash. Between your speed and your shifting magic, you're one of a kind! You just had to believe in yourself."

Flash grinned from ear to ear. "I couldn't have done it without my teammate," she said, nudging Twinkle. "You showed me that I didn't need to be scared of messing up!"

Twinkle gave a dramatic bow and laughed. "Happy to be of service!"

The last few minutes of the game went by in a blur. Both teams played hard, but no one else scored. When Mr. Magictail blew the final whistle, the score was 9–7.

Bow wow—the Maroon Team had won the Cutie Bowl!

Chapter 10

"Barking Bulldogs, it's like a sea of maroon and gold!" Sparkle cried, stepping out into the school courtyard the next day.

The pups had finished a morning of magic lessons, and now the final celebration of Spirit Week was about to begin! Pups as far as the eye could see were dressed in maroon and gold, the Cutiecorn Academy school colors. Flash had worn her favorite school baseball cap, plus a striped sweater. Her friends were decked out in scarves, sweatshirts, vests, floppy hats—just about any maroon and gold clothing they could get their paws on!

Flash sniffed the air. "I can't focus on anything but that puptastic smell!" she said, her eyes wide. "I love a good barbecue!" As if on cue, her stomach rumbled loudly.

Sparkle, Glitter, and Twinkle all laughed. "Leave it to Flash to focus on the food during Spirit Week," Twinkle joked.

Glitter took a deep breath. "Mmmm, I think Flash is right! Those burgers smell totally furbulous."

Once the four friends got their burgers

(and piled them high with yummy toppings), they wandered over to eat in front of the stage. The Magic Mutts, Flash's favorite band, was set up there for a concert to celebrate the last day of Spirit Week!

"I can't wait for the music to start," Flash said around a mouthful of food. "I have some new dance moves to try out!"

"Is one of them called 'Belly Full of Burger'?" Sparkle joked.

Flash did a silly move, sticking her belly out and twirling in a circle. She got so dizzy she fell snout-first on the ground, laughing so hard she could hardly catch her breath.

"Attention, students!" Mrs. Horne's voice crackled over the microphone just then, and

Flash got back to her paws, popping the last of her burger into her mouth and trying to stifle her giggles.

Mrs. Horne waved from up on the stage. "What a truly pawsome week we've had!" The crowd of pups cheered. "You've all demonstrated lots of spirit and magic this week, and Cutiecorn Academy is lucky to have each and every one of you. I know we're all eager for the concert to begin, but I'd like to hand out a few special awards first."

Flash looked at her friends with wide eyes. Awards?

"Every year, we like to acknowledge the pup with the most school spirit," Mrs. Horne said. "I think you'll all agree that Sprinkles has earned that title!"

The crowd began barking up a storm as a Yellow Lab with a dark green horn made her way to the stage. She was dressed in maroon and gold from snout to paws, and Flash recognized her as the pup who had led all the biggest chants and cheers during the Cutie Bowl. Flash clapped and woofed as Sprinkles took a dramatic bow and accepted her award.

"Next, the Magnificent Magic award," Mrs. Horne went on. "This goes to the pup who shows mastery of their magical skills over the course of the week. This year, that pup is Roxy!" The Sheltie who had won the obstacle course on Monday ran onto the stage. Flash admired her energy and spunk—maybe she'd be like Roxy in a few years!

Mrs. Horne held up a paw for quiet as

Roxy left the stage. "Finally, our Cutie Bowl MVP! This pup showed persistence, determination, and some barking good magical skills. This is all the more impressive because she's a first-year student. Congratulations, Flash!"

Holy bones, had Mrs. Horne just said *her* name?

Sparkle, Twinkle, and Glitter all began jumping up and down, patting her on the back and barking up a storm. Flash was frozen in place, shocked.

Glitter placed a gentle paw on her back and nudged her toward the front. "Go on, Flash! Mrs. Horne is waiting for you."

Dazed, Flash walked up onto the stage and accepted her MVP trophy from Mrs. Horne. She was going to remember this moment furever!

As she turned to leave, Mrs. Horne held
up a paw. "Hold on just a minute, Flash. As
everyone knows, first-year students receive
charms for their bracelets each time they reach
new magical milestones. I'd like to invite the
rest of the first-year pups up here to get their
Spirit Week charms!"

Before Flash knew it, the rest of her class had joined her onstage, wiggling with excitement.

Mrs. Horne held out a pawful of sparkling gold charms shaped like tiny footballs. "You'll always have these to commemorate your first Spirit Week! You all used your magic in new and wonderful ways this week. You should be puptastically proud of yourselves!" She fastened a charm onto each pup's bracelet.

As she walked off the stage with her friends, Flash couldn't help admiring her beautiful, jingly charm bracelet. It shimmered in the afternoon sun like magic.

Just then, the Magic Mutts struck up a tune. It was concert time!

"Here, let me take that for you," Sparkle

said, holding out a paw for Flash's MVP trophy. She winked. "You're going to need your paws free for dancing!"

SEE HOW THE ADVENTURE BEGAN IN
HEART OF GOLD

Chapter 1

"Bow wow, Sparkle, that was puptastic!" Twinkle cheered, clapping her paws. On either side of her, her friends Glitter and Flash barked and whooped in agreement.

Up onstage, Sparkle took a graceful bow. Her golden fur shimmered in the spotlight— and so did the golden horn between her ears. After all, Sparkle, Twinkle, and their friends weren't regular puppies. They were Cutiecorns! The colorful horns on their heads gave them pawsome magical powers. But Sparkle had just wowed them with no magic at all!

"I had no idea you could sing like that!" Glitter said, giving Sparkle a hug as she stepped down from the stage.

"Me neither," Flash barked, racing in excited circles. "That was incrediwoof!"

Sparkle blushed, but a happy smile stretched across her snout. "Thanks! I've been practicing doggone hard."

"This talent show is going to be the best thing Puppypaw Island has ever seen!" Flash cried. "Just think how impressed our visitors will be!"

Twinkle couldn't help grinning at her

friend's enthusiasm. Flash never missed an opportunity to yap on and on about something! Even though Twinkle pretended to be grumpy about it sometimes, it was one of the things she liked best about the little Yorkshire Terrier—she was a bundle of energy and excitement! Plus, the talent show was definitely something to bark about.

"It *is* pretty ter-ruff-ic that we get to host Cutiecorns from far and wide this weekend," Twinkle said with a nod.

Sparkle danced on her paws. "Yup, turns out something good did come from those mischievous little kittens who showed up here! Everyone wants to get to know one another a little better," she said. "The first-ever

Cutiecorn Carnival and Talent Show is going to be a grrrrrreat success. I just know it!"

Twinkle peered around the auditorium from her seat in the first row. In front of her was an impressive stage with heavy red curtains and bright lights. Behind her, rows of padded seats stretched on and on into the darkness. Of all the rooms at the pups' school, Cutiecorn Academy, Twinkle thought this one must be the grandest. It was nice of Mrs. Horne, the head of the school, to let them stay after and practice on the big stage!

"My turn," Glitter said quietly, climbing up the steps. She cued some music, took a deep breath, and began dancing, twirling, and leaping across the stage. Twinkle knew that her friend had been taking ballet lessons ever since she was a little pup, but she'd had no idea that Glitter had turned into such a barking good ballerina!

Sparkle and Flash both looked at Twinkle with wide eyes. They were surprised, too!

When the music faded, Glitter posed pawfectly still for a moment. Then she curtsied as her friends erupted into a flurry of barks and cheers.

"You're so graceful!"

"Hot dog, what a performance!"

"You're a puptastic ballerina!"

This time, it was Glitter's turn to blush as she stepped down from the stage. "I love to dance," she said with a happy sigh. "It's my favorite thing in the whole world!"

About the Author

Shannon Penney doesn't have any magical powers, but she has ter-ruff-ic fun writing about them! If she were a Cutiecorn, she'd have a turquoise horn and the ability to turn everything to ice cream. For now, she'll settle for the ice and snow of New Hampshire, where she writes, edits, and goes on adventures with her husband, two kids, and their non-magical cat.